Millions of Americans remember Dick and Jane (and Sally and Spot too!). The little stories with their simple vocabulary words and warmly rendered illustrations were a hallmark of American education in the 1950s and 1960s.

But the first Dick and Jane stories actually appeared much earlier—in the Scott Foresman Elson Basic Reader Pre-Primer, copyright 1930. These books featured short, upbeat, and highly readable stories for children. The pages were filled with colorful characters and large, easy-to-read Century Schoolbook typeface. There were fun adventures around every corner of Dick and Jane's world.

Generations of American children learned to read with Dick and Jane, and many still cherish the memory of reading the simple stories on their own. Today, Pearson Scott Foresman remains committed to helping all children learn to read—and love to read. As part of Pearson Education, the world's largest educational publisher, Pearson Scott Foresman is honored to reissue these classic Dick and Jane stories, with Grosset & Dunlap, a division of Penguin Young Readers Group. Reading has always been at the heart of everything we do, and we sincerely hope that reading is an important part of your life too.

Dick and Jane is a registered trademark of Addison-Wesley Educational Publishers, Inc.
From THE NEW WE LOOK AND SEE. Copyright © 1956 by Scott, Foresman and Company,
copyright renewed 1984. From THE NEW WE WORK AND PLAY. Copyright © 1956 by
Scott, Foresman and Company, copyright renewed 1984. From THE NEW WE COME AND
GO. Copyright © 1956 by Scott, Foresman and Company, copyright renewed 1984. All rights
reserved. Published in 2004 by Grosset & Dunlap, a division of Penguin Young Readers Group,
345 Hudson Street, New York, NY, 10014. GROSSET & DUNLAP is a trademark of Penguin
Group (USA) Inc. Published simultaneously in Canada. Printed in the U.S.A.

Library of Congress Cataloging-in-Publication Data
We see.
    p. cm. — (Read with Dick and Jane ; 9)
    Summary: A collection of classic Dick and Jane stories in which they play with Sally, Tim,
Spot, and Puff, and spy cars, boats, and other interesting objects.
    ISBN 0-448-43408-3 (pbk.) — ISBN 0-448-43494-6 (hardcover)
    [1. Play—Fiction. 2. Pets—Fiction. 3. Vehicles—Fiction. 4. Vocabulary.] I. Series.
PZ7.W35143 2004
[E]—dc22   2003016829

ISBN 0-448-43494-6 (GB)   A B C D E F G H I J
ISBN 0-448-43408-3 (pbk)   A B C D E F G H I J

Read with
Dick and Jane

We See

GROSSET & DUNLAP • NEW YORK

Look and See

Look, Spot.

Look, Puff.

Look and see.

See Sally and Tim.

Come, Spot, come.

Jump up.

See Puff jump.

Jump up, Spot.

Jump up.

Come, Dick, come.

Come and see.

See Tim.

See Spot and Puff.

Look, Dick, look.

The Little Car

Oh, oh, oh.

See my red car.

See my yellow car.

Come, Father, come.

Help Baby Sally.

Oh, Father.

I see my blue car.

I see my yellow car.

Look, Father, look.

Find my little red car.

Help Sally find the red car.

Look, Father.

I see the red car.

I can find the little red car.

See my cars.

Red and blue and yellow.

Red and blue and yellow cars.

Tim and Baby Sally

Sally said, "Oh, Tim.

I see something.

Mother sees something.

Dick and Jane see something."

"Oh, oh," said Sally.

"I see something.

Something for Baby Sally.

And something for little Tim."

Sally said, "I see something.
Something for Dick and Jane.
And something for Sally.
I want something for Tim."

"Oh, look," said Dick.

"See something for little Tim."

Spot and Puff

Baby Sally said, "Look here.
I see something funny.
I see Spot and little Puff.
Spot wants something.
Puff wants something."

Jane said, "Look, Mother.
See Spot and Puff.
Spot and Puff want something."

Mother said, "Run, Jane.
Run, Dick.
Run and help little Sally.
Sally wants help."

"Oh, oh," said Baby Sally.

"Oh.

　　　Oh.

　　　　　Oh."

I See Three

"Here, Dick," said Mother.
"Here is something."

"I see three," said Dick.
"We want three.
I want a big one.
Jane wants a big one.
Sally wants a little one."

"One, two, three," said Jane.
"A big one for Dick.
A big one for Jane.
A little one for Baby Sally.
One, two, three."

"Oh, oh," said Sally.
"One, two, three.
One, two, three."

"See, see," said Father.
"One, two, three.
I see something funny."

"Run, run," said Sally
"Here we come."

Father said, "Oh, oh.
Here I go."

The Blue Boat

Jane said, "See the red boat.
See the yellow boat."

Dick said, "I see two blue boats.
Two little blue boats."

Sally said, "I see the boats.
A big yellow boat.
A little red boat.
And two blue boats.
Yellow, red, and blue."

"Oh, my," said Baby Sally.

"Tim is not here.

Where is Tim?

Oh, Jane.

Help me.

Help me find Tim."

"Look, Baby Sally," said Jane.
"See Spot jump in.
Spot can find Tim for you."

"Oh, oh," said Dick.
"See Spot go."

"Here comes Spot," said Jane.

"Here comes Spot to the boat."

"Oh, oh," said Baby Sally.
"Here comes Spot.
And here comes Tim."